Rachel and the Golden Glasses

Eileen Bell

"W hen all is said and done,
the weather and love are the two
elements about which one can never be
sure."
— Alice Hoffman, Here on Earth

Rachel and the Golden Glasses

By Eileen Bell

ISBN: 978-1-989092-71-2

Celticfrog Publishing
Clearwater, BC

Rachel is standing on the steps of the family home, "Cliff-Side," screaming, "Come away Grandpa, Come away!"

The old man stands parallel to the edge of the cliff. He is bending down to retrieve a small object from the ground. Then, after successfully recovering the object, attempts to step sideways, away from the imminent danger; from the swirling mouth of the sea below and the insistent lightning above. He sways a little towards the precipice, his long frame only a foggy shadow, his beard a thick, drooping mass from the end of his chin and the relentless rain pelting against his sodden cloak.

Rachel's heart shudders.

He takes a few steps away from the edge of the cliff. He carefully places the object in a pocket inside his cloak. He then looks down at his soggy beard. He wrings it forcefully between his fingers releasing the dirty water onto the ground, as grandma would wring a dirty mop into the wash bucket. Then he moves his faltering feet towards the house. Before he reaches the step where Rachel stands, he takes the item from his cloak pocket. As he looks up at Rachel, she sees he is wearing a small pair of wire-rimmed, yellow-green tinted glasses. They hang over the edge of his nose and his eyes above which are a deeper, more intense green than the glasses, are clearly speaking to her. *Watch me now my child,* they seem to be saying. He then turns and faces the crackling sky, the wind, and the rumbling trees. He mumbles a few words Rachel can't make out. The wind halts suddenly. Then the sky's mesmerizing network of electrical waves fizzle into nothingness. The rain drains to a few miserable drops running down Rachel's neck and puddling into her dress. The fog lifts to reveal a patch of thin blue below the emerging milky clouds. A potent silence then, as in the aftermath of a prayer. God's creation about to renew itself and perhaps needing to ponder how to begin this important task.

Without warning, a slash of wind blows the old man backwards and sends him sailing through the air like a broken branch, arms outstretched, over the cliff and to the depths below. The gust stops as suddenly as it began. All is eerily silent once again. Rachel screams in horror, her hands over her mouth, frozen on the steps and then after a few unaccountable minutes walks as if in a trance, towards the cliff. The glasses are lying on the ground a short distance from the cliff. She almost trips over them. She reaches down to pick them up, but knows better than to put them on. Her head no longer feels foggy. Everything is all too real. She peers over the cliff in horror. She can scarcely find the outline of her beloved grandpa's crumpled body in the jumble of rocks and debris below. She knows he is down below- forever lost and she knows he is dead. Grandpa, Grandpa!! she screams over and over. Her heart is shattering.

Her mother, Emily, finds her passed out, lying near the cliff edge in her thin cotton dress, the glasses beside her. She recovers the glasses from the wet ground. Emily, shivering and shaking with grief, carries her daughter home, cradling her in her arms, weeping over her. Parting her hair and kissing her wet face. Later she lies quietly beside the sleeping child in the dark, never moving, not taking her eyes from the face of the small ten year old girl. Rachel recovers, but like her mother is never the same again. From the trauma of watching her grandfather fall to his death over the cliff, she acquired a morbid fear of going anywhere near the cliff or any other high space overlooking the sea, much to her mother's relief. Her mother puts the glasses away. Out of sight, out of mind. Life carries on.

Rachel attends school in the village. She weeds the garden and tends the goats with her mother on the weekends. She plays school-yard games and after school throws pebbles and skips along the worn gravel and dirt road with her friends. They skip past the family farms and apple orchards, similar to their own orchard and garden property; Rachel and Emily's only source of income. All properties border the narrow road, each property is 4-5 acres of fertile land bordering the ocean, along the western edge of Vancouver Island. Rachel remembers grandfather telling her when she was a child, that if her eyes one day become strong enough, she might see across the salt water to Japan.

She loses all interest in faraway places.

As the years go by, Rachel grows long- legged and restless. She walks by herself in the nearby woods or rides their mare, Sally, at a thunderous thud down the road. She lies in the meadow just past the school. Rachel chews lazily on a piece of grass, her curly, red hair spread out over the thick green canopy as the mare grazes beside her. She looks at the dense blue sky through a shimmering haze of

August heat. She had learned in school that the sun produces a kind of gravity that is also affected by the changes in the atmosphere.

The sky feels so heavy, like it will fall right into my lap.

She shades her eyes and squints through the waves of heat up to the blistering sun. She thinks often of her grandpa. The glasses were a part of him and if she could just hold them once again, she wouldn't miss him so much. *Maybe I could work some magic with my eyes alone, break through the veils without any stupid old glasses. Why were Forestt Fineman's and my eyes the same colour as the glasses? Any glasses are just an extension of a working eyeball, are they not?* She sits up and stares ahead unblinking, still chewing on the blade of grass. *Who am I kidding? My mother's eyes are green and my grandpa's were more yellow. Heredity is all that is. Who knows about my father's eyes? Who knows about my father? Mother never tells me anything.*

***

Eileen Bell

1965

Rachel is sixteen.

During the weary summer days, Emily and Rachel often argue.

"The glasses, the glasses. That's all you want to talk about."

"The glasses are not to blame."

"Who or what else is to blame then, my child? Not your grandpa, Forestt. I tell you the glasses have an evil side. They have prevented a lot of bad weather, but look, why did they bring back the wind that blew Grandpa away? Can you answer that?"
Rachel trembled. She didn't like going against her mother's wishes, but she knew inexplicably she was right. She also knew one day she would possess the glasses.

"Maybe it was just a freak of nature beyond any control. The glasses can't be evil by themselves, they are only a tool to help control weather."

"Freak of nature, alright. Those yellow-green-eyed glasses are a freak of nature. Look at your yellow-
6

green eyes. You are a child. Look in the mirror. You don't know the story."

"Then tell me the story! Put down that dam smoke mom! This is the '60's, not the 1940's. Parents actually talk to their kids about stuff now and I have a right to know and understand things for myself." She wrings her hands. Her hair hangs over her eyes and two sloppy tears grace her cheek. She wipes them away with the back of her hand. "I love you mum. I'm pleading with you. I have to know. Am I a freak of nature too, because my eyes are yellow-green like the glasses? Is that what you're saying. Am I some horrible reminder to you of what happened to Grandpa? He lived his life as he chose just like I wish to do. Maybe there was some will of his own in his flying backwards over the cliff."

"How can you say such a horrible thing. Why do you think such thoughts?" She takes a long drag from her cigarette. Shaking with anger she collapses into the nearest chair. She lights another smoke but then quickly butts it in the ashtray on the coffee table. Her hands shake. Then straightening herself, she leans closer to Rachel. Her tone is softer, but her eyes are full of anger.

"Go away from me! Go away from me!" You are not my child to say a thing like this about your grandfather."

Rachel runs out slamming the front door.

Emily immediately regrets talking harshly and calls from the doorway after her daughter.

 She cups her hands around her mouth and shouts after her. "Please come back. I didn't mean I wanted you to leave—" She falters over the last words, "—our home. Rachel, Rachel. I love you." she shouts as Rachel disappears down the dirt road to leading into town."

She returns to grab her smoke from the ashtray by the chair and leans over the porch railing, dragging deep on her cigarette and watching Rachel disappear around the first bend in the road.

"Perhaps she'll just talk it out with a friend and be home later."

***

Rachel does not come home.

She hitch-hikes south, down the island highway with the ache of anger in her heart, and no real destination in mind. Hungry and exhausted, she decides to stop in a town on the sea edge called Port David. She is directed by a passerby to trendy site bordering an inlet. She is accepted into a loose-knit camp at Delphina Beach. The camp is looked after by a scattered group of long haired kids with loose, shabby clothes only a few years older than her. They ask very few questions, and a young man directs her to a shelter propped up by cedar poles, and covered in canvas

 "No booze. This ain't no old hobo camp," says the tall young man with a friendly smile. He points behind him "If you need anything there's the food shack where we cook and give out fresh seafood, when it's available, and produce from our garden. We always need people to work the garden, clean and cook. Whatever's goin' down." Outhouses are a distance from the camp on the far bank. If you want to bathe there's the ocean. We're all free here. Don't need no booze and we don't need bathing suits." He snickers and looks her up and down with a smile that's a little too friendly, then shrugs and turns back to his friends who are sitting in a ragged circle strumming guitars, passing around a joint and talking.

A few mop-haired children dance and play in the sand nearby. A couple of dogs run in circles barking and chasing each other and the children. A man and a woman are standing quietly, waist deep in the ocean, water sliding and glistening off naked arms and backs in the late afternoon sun. She spots a man alone in a wooden boat out in the ocean, fishing with a crooked pole and a string. She turns away from the beach and the hippies, into her canvas shelter.

Within a few days she befriends an older man named Ralph who lives in the hut next to hers. One morning they sit side by side on two cracked plastic chairs outside Ralph's makeshift driftwood and cedar shack.

Rachel takes to him almost right away. She finds herself telling him about the horrible accident when she was ten and her mother hiding the glasses and then refusing, in the years afterwards, to discuss anything about her grandfather with her. She knows she needs a friend, a stranger like Ralph who has no connection to her life. This felt safe. As safe as anyone can be, living on the ocean shore in a canvas and plastic lean-to, wearing the same clothes every day, and depending on handouts for food.

"I miss my mother and my friends from the village," she tells Ralph.

He speaks in a thin rasping voice, alternately puffing on a well-worn butt and coughing into the back of his hand. He sweeps a few strands of straggly hair away from his face.

"Go back home. You are still a child. Your mother must be hurt and angry. She don't want you livin' like this. Me... I got the cancer or somethin' like that in my throat." He rubs a long spindly hand over his Adam's apple, which hung loosely against the ropy muscles in his neck. "Can't hardly talk sometimes, hurts so bad. You notice."

Rachel shivers at being referred to as a child, but because she feels sympathy for the old man, says nothing.

"What's 'is name? Your grandfather."

"Forestt Fineman."

His hand trembles. He drops the butt into the sand and steps on it, then speaks slowly and carefully. "Forest, you say?" Forestt with a double t?"

Ralph sits, staring ahead, lost, Rachel thinks, in another world. He then shifts in his chair, leans towards Rachel. He speaks in a conspiratorial whisper, his hand to the side of his mouth. "Likely I knew him back in the day when life meant somethin'. He had eyes the same colour as you. You got them golden- green eyes too. Must be a connection."

He throws back his head and laughs.

"What?" Rachel stands up knocking over her chair, kicking it aside. Incredulity written all over her face. She stands with hands on her hips facing him, her eyes fixed steadily on him. "You crazy old man. Are you telling me this cause you got nothing better to do with your time. You making it up for entertainment? This isn't funny. This is my life."

She stomps off, but feels her anger thwarted and not a little foolish, when her sandals drag across the beach. Rachel sits and sighs, looking out over the ocean and scrapes the sand from the soles of her sandals with a stick.

She wishes Ralph hadn't noticed her eyes. How could he possibly know about her Grandpa's eyes? She pokes at the cold sand with the stick.

Ralph follows Rachel and sits on the sand a short distance from her. He looks towards her with a weary smile.

"We'd better get you some decent shoes. Winter's comin'."

 Staring fixedly at the ocean, hands across her knees. Her jaw is tight and her throat aches with bitterness.

"Like you care." She pauses, sighs, begins again. "Don't you see. I can't go home til I find out the truth about his life. How do I know you aren't just trying to get something from me?"

"I have nothing left to gain or lose. Look at me. I'm a sick old man in a hippie camp. They take me like I am here, as I'm no longer lookin' for pride, love nor money. This keeps me real honest. Maybe even closer to God if you believe in that stuff," he answers with a short laugh. "The only thing left for me is to try and help others if I can. It sometimes even keeps me from the bottle. Suits me. They don't like no drinkin' here. They like them skinny cigarettes that make them silly in the head for a bit and then sleepy."

He looks at Rachel sheepishly and shrugs, scrounges a dirty butt from his pocket, lights it with a match and leans toward her with a mocking, waggish grin. "If I run out of smokes, I can always smoke up with the kids." He turns and waves his arm towards the young people milling around outside the food hut.

She smiles begrudgingly at Ralph, as an understanding passes between them.

***

"Back in the days we knew each other. Forestt, your grandfather, wrote a children's story about a pair of green- yellow tinted glasses found by a young boy on his way home from school. Maybe he got the idea, because he always wondered why his eyes were such a strange colour. The child in the story discovers the glasses can change the weather, but only if he believes they can. Save people from a lot of destruction and disaster. That's what starts it all. He had this theory that if you write something and totally believe what you've written it will morph into reality or reveal the reality already present, even if it's a made-up story. Is art life or life art? That's where he began with it all. He made those glasses himself."

Really, Ralph. Rachel wants to blurt out, *Is this another story?* She decides instead to act like she believes him and stay in focus.

 "Where," Rachel asks taking a deep breath, trying to keep her voice from squeaking with the high-pitched excitement that made her legs tingle and her stomach flutter, "is the book now?"

"See ya' here tomorrow – we'll talk – same time. I'm not sayin' I can help. I'm a tired old man near the end of my life, need to rest now."

***

The next day Rachel waits in the chair for Ralph. *It is not like he lives so far away or has to drive through traffic.* So she walks to his hut and pokes her head inside. She calls his name, but he doesn't answer. He is sprawled on the makeshift bed, as if in a peaceful sleep, books spread out around him. Rachel touches his shoulder.

She touches his forehead, then leans over to hear if he is breathing. The stench of death wafts over her.

Rachel stumbles backwards onto the rough planked floor. She sits with head in hand. Her gut rumbles with nausea and a slow simmering anger. She stands up and begins kicking at whatever is near. Ralph's boots fly through the doorway; a tattered writing desk, thick with scattered papers and an unsteady leg implodes after she gives it a fierce kick. Then she turns her anger to the lifeless body on the bed.

"Why now, Ralph why now?" she screams at the lifeless body. "I just met you two weeks ago and now you're dead. Where's the book? Couldn't you at least have told me where it was before you croaked?"

Then a wave of compassion for Ralph, for herself, for her mom and her grandfather sweeps over her and she begins to weep. She lies on the floor by the crumpled desk and weeps uncontrollably. As her crying lessens, she sits up, wiping her eyes. She looks down at the floor. The planks widen and sink under her weight. There is soft earth under the sagging boards. She lifts two of the boards and pushes them aside. The first thing she discovers is a satchel full of books in this hole Ralph had dug. She lugs the heavy satchel up from the hole and over to a small table by the door. She also notices an unmarked envelope sticking out from one of the books. *I'd better replace the boards before I look at anything else. Don't want others nosing around in here. That's my job.* Curiosity and the faintest glimmering of hope overtake her. She wipes away the last of her tears. She replaces the boards carefully. *This day is getting really interesting. What do I do about his body? I wanted to uncover a mystery. So here it begins.*

Rachel peers out the door of the hut. It's starting to drizzle warm rain. She hauls the bag of books off the table and leaves the hut dragging the satchel. She shuffles it to her own small enclosure. She pulls a makeshift curtain across the entrance and opens the envelope. Inside is a broken string of polished silver beads which she cradles in her hand. She sets them in a small dish on the table and then pulls a crumpled paper from the envelope. It reads:

> You'll find this letter on my death. I
> am your father, Ralph Fineman, only
> son of Forestt. Emily Green, your
> mother and I were only married for a
> few beautiful years. I left Cliff-Side

under unfortunate circumstances, of
my own choosing, when you were two.
I returned briefly a few times after my
father was blown off the cliff, but,
sadly, I didn't see you. So here you are
you are, Rachel Green-Forestt and you
are indeed like a beautiful green forest
ready to begin life on your own terms.
I hoped to know you much longer dear
child, but as I write this, I know I am
not long for this world.

Rachel looks at the date. She blurts out her words,
as if he was in her room.

"Ralph, Ralph..You wrote this letter only yesterday.
The strain of burying this note and the books must
have weakened you – helped to bring on your
death."

Her heart pounding with sorrow and excitement,
she continues reading the scratchy, pencilled hand
on the next page.

My darling Rachel,
The necklace is worth a bit of money
so it will help you leave the camp and
begin your own life. I'm askin' you to

take this note to your mother. You are
still very young, so sit down with her
and talk about what you both might do
next. The necklace is yours and it is
yours to do with as you wish. Leave
my body as is. The members of the
camp will find it and call the
authorities. If you tell them who you
are they may alert the child welfare, as
you are still legally a child. I know you
must be feelin' pretty mixed up right
now. The book my father Forestt was
writin' that started the business with
the weather glasses is in the satchel.
Show this book to your mother. It may
help her to tell you what she knows of
how it played out. Now the story is up
to you and Emily.

Life is mysterious. What led you to
stumble alone and hungry to this camp?
I had nothing to do with it. Your
mother would not talk to me or let me
visit in all those years, so I had no idea
that you had run from Cliff-Side.

I listened to you talking of the death of
Forestt yesterday and how you as a ten

year old kid looked on at his tragic and
still unexplained death. You became ill
because of what happened and when
you recovered from the illness, began
to obsess, understandably, over the
reason for the glasses not working
when they should have protected your
grandfather. I was troubled to hear your
account of his death, but at the same
time beyond happy to know finally that
I had, by a beautiful accident, found
my daughter.

"You are the last and most beautiful
gift of my life. I did have to leave you
yesterday, much as I hated to, as I
could not contain my feelings with you
beside me. This has been the happiest
and also the saddest day of my life.
All my earthly love is for you. I leave
you now. Go well.
Ralph Fineman.

The book... The book. She wipes away helpless
tears brought on by the beauty and loneliness of the
letter she had just read. Nonetheless, she feels
impatient to get her hands on her grandfather's
book. She dumps the contents of the satchel onto

the table. *There it is.* "Ralph and the Golden Glasses." The cover is tattered and dirty, but it shimmers as if it is alive. Golden green and a hint of blue, she says out-loud. *It's as if the book was waiting for me to find it.* She sits, lays it on the table and opens it. The first line of the first page reads.

> Ralph changes the weather on Tuesday
> the 25th of April, while he is walking
> home from school. It is an ordinary day,
> but there are a few dark clouds on the
> edge of the sky.

Then she looks at the title and sees a picture of a boy on the second page walking down a city street carrying a pack over his arm and rattling a stick along a wooden fence. On the opposite page it reads.

> Ralph sees the dark clouds. He doesn't
> want it to rain because he is excited
> about playing softball in the vacant lot
> with his friends. Then he sees a dirty
> pair of glasses lying in the ditch by the
> fence. He picks them up and puts them
> on. At this moment, the world as he
> knows it changes.

She reads the story to the end, then cradles the book against her chest, as if embracing a cherished friend. Then she places it carefully back in the satchel.

Oh my God, he wrote this book for Ralph when he was a boy. The pieces of the puzzle are starting to fit together. I have to get out of here, go home and show Mom Ralph's letter. I won't show her the necklace though and maybe not the book either. I have to think about this. What will I do about his body? He is my father. I can't just leave him here. My mother will have to check out the body. What a mess this all is. Oh, but it's all so wonderful too! I have to fix things with mom like Ralph asked. There are so many things to fix.

***

The next day Rachel walks down the road away from the camp, her backpack full with Ralph's books her few clothes, the necklace and the letter, She turns at the entrance and looks back at the scattered outpost. She sighs, walks hurriedly away heading towards the town centre.

The night before Rachel huddled under her thin blankets and eats her few remaining bits of food. She talks out loud. This helps her feel less alone.

"I'll go to the police station and try to explain the situation. I'll be brief. I'll ask if I can call my mother. Oh my God, what will I say? Oh Mom, can you come and see to Dad's body. Yes, he died in a homeless camp where I was staying. I have to start somewhere. She is the only one who can identify his body. Maybe I can hang around til she gets here and I'll go home with her after. I'll see how things go."

Rachel, knees trembling, walks up to the wicket in the small police station. A shrivelled receptionist turns around, looking annoyed at being roused from her typewriter, a damp cigarette dangling from her lip. She pulls the cigarette carefully from her mouth as if she is peeling a bandage off her skin, and places it still smouldering in an ashtray next to a cup of long standing coffee. She peers through the bars at Rachel as if she is checking on a jailbird, except she is the one behind the bars.

"How cin I help." She grimaces.
"I want to report a dead body."
"Gimme a name. Gimme your name."
"He's my father. I think."

The little grey woman turns in her chair and picks the butt of the cigarette from the ashtray, straightens it out and places it between her lips, as if arming herself. "Ya' don't know your own dad?"

"Long story."

"I bet'cha it is," she cackles. "SARGENT!" She bellows towards the back room. "She says her dad's dead. Don't know why she's here. Underage. Likely a run-away. You better look at this one."

Relieved to be away from the screaming woman, Rachel follows the portly officer to the back room.

He looks friendly enough. Rachel dumps her backpack on the floor. She sits across from the Sargent and tries to explain. "I am-was in a camp. I met my dad... at least I think so."

He looks at her, his wide brow furrowed with concern. "Let's start with a name. Yours."

"Rachel Green Fineman."

"Your dad's name?"

"Ralph Fineman." She sits tall in her chair and tries hard to sound sensible and grown-up but her face is streaked with dirt and tears. "He's dead in his hut in

24

the camp on Delphina Beach. I have been staying in the camp. I found him yesterday morning. We were supposed to meet. Can you call my mother, Emily Green? She can identify the body. I can show her. Please can I call her?"

Rachel shivers and tries to wipe her face with the back of her hand.

"How do you know he's your dad?"

"He told me so and I believe him. We only met in the camp a week or so ago. I know it sounds crazy and weird."

"Did you bring his ID?"

"Oh, I never thought."

"I need to see your ID."

She digs in her backpack and finds her crumpled ID card and a pen with which she scrawls her mother's phone number. She pushes them in front of the cop.

The officer looks intently at the card, then stands up, his face poker straight. He pushes his chair back.

"Okay, Rachel Green or Green-Fineman or whoever you are, this is what we're gonna do. I'm gonna call your mother. You sit here."

A few minutes later he returns. "Rachel Green, the dead body you have reported to have found will be picked up and taken to the local morgue and your mother will identify the body in a few days. Meanwhile, you're going home to Cliff-Side."

***

Rachel is alone in the house one winter afternoon a few months after she returns home. She stands staring up the ladder to the attic and speaks out-loud to the empty space around her. "How long am I going to stay a whining wimp. How long am I going to let what happened to grandfather make me a coward? Mom and I buried Ralph in the family plot last week, next to the memorial to grandfather. We wept, said prayers. We bonded over our shared loss. It's time to check out where the glasses are. Mom is not likely to tell me now."

Her gut wrenches and she is dizzy. She's had an inkling for awhile, that the attic must be where her mom hid the glasses, which makes sense, as long as Rachel is still afraid of heights. "I've hitch-hiked down the island, hung out in a homeless camp, met up with my father whom I helped bury last week. I should be able to climb a ladder without fainting." Rachel takes a step onto the ladder with her right foot. Then her left. Both feet now on the first rung. She stands there for a moment staring up at the hole into the attic. "Nowhere to go but up." She grabs the side of the ladder firmly. When she reaches the top she is breathless, not from exertion, but from her own sense of accomplishment.

With a thrust of her arms, Rachel propels herself through the attic opening and slides sideways, halfway across the room. She lies there smiling and staring at the roof, pulling at the strands of dust coating her mouth, feeling like she'd limped over the finish line of a race with blistered feet. She sits up coughing and wiping bits from her teeth.

"Where would mom hide the glasses from a small child? I better find them before she gets home. I don't want her freaking out." She stands and looks over some objects sitting on a shelf easily at her eye level. A golden coloured glass box catches her eye. She opens it. All it contains is a scrap of paper. She reads.

> When you find this box Rachel, you
> will know where to find the glasses.
> Love your father, Ralph.

"What!! How insane. Ralph how could you play games with something so important? She shouts at the lonely attic walls. "This is not a child's treasure hunt. Are you haunting me from beyond the grave?" Rachel screams in frustration and throws the box. It lands heavily against the wall and shatters. Then she perches on the child size bench and thinks. *This means Ralph knew who I was as soon as he noticed me at Delphinia Beach. He was here in the house after grandfather died. He was the one who hid the glasses! Why? I have to find them now!*

Looking across the room she notices a small gold key lying among the shards of yellow glass. Picking it up she sees it has a tiny, faded piece of paper taped to the back with an address— 333 Windless Lane. PD. She gasps.

"Port-David! Is this where the glasses are, in a house in Port- David? Is this what Ralph was saying in his first note? The more I learn the more mysterious and tangled this web becomes. "Windless Lane"? Sounds like an address in a fairy tale. Do fairy tales have addresses? Is it possible that mom really doesn't know where the glasses are? Why then was Ralph, if he had a home in Port-David, living in a hippie camp? This has to be another family home of Ralph's. I wonder if Mom knows about this?"

Rachel brushes debris from her jeans and shirt. She picks up the shards of glass and places them in a little pot on the shelf. She shoves the key and the scrap of paper with the note from Ralph into her jeans pocket. Taking the pot with the broken glass in hand, she makes her way carefully down the ladder to the hallway then pushes the ladder back up into its slotted space in the ceiling. She hides the small pot with the glass in a corner cupboard in her bedroom before sprawling across her bed, revelling in her adventure.

I'll have to find my way back to Port- David to see if this key still fits the front door. I can't risk telling Mom anything more right now. I feel like such a cheat, a deceiver. But this is my chance to find out what really happened. Maybe one day I will be able to control the weather with the glasses as grandfather did. She sees the irony in the situation. *Maybe not quite like grandfather.*

***

In late June of 1966, Rachel knocks gingerly on the door of 333 Windless Lane. She approached the house from the back. The house number is on the back door, or is this the front? *Everything is different here. It's like own little magical kingdom separate from the rest of the town.*

She has been researching everything she can about weather systems ever since she found the clues to the whereabouts of the glasses in the attic. She has learned a lot regarding solar radiation and so on, but no answers as to why a short street in a mid-island town bordering the ocean, would experience very little or no wind. *Who named the street? Maybe it was a joke? If the name is not a joke it must be very hot here*, she thinks as she walks down the narrow lane towards number 333. The lane-way is scattered with small assorted pebbles No soft sand to absorb heat and encourage a breeze from the ocean. The narrow lane is lined on either side with wispy yellow and green willow trees whose branches join together loosely in a canopy overhead.

A short dark haired young girl, several years younger, answers the door. "How can I help you?" she says politely. She is dressed in jeans and a t-shirt, and her hair is long and loose. Rachel had never thought about what she would say when this moment arrived. "My name is Rachel. I have a key to your house. Not sure which door it fits. Found it in my mother's attic. I have a job in Port David for the summer. Can I come in?"

"Ah-h yeah. My name is Sylvia. Yeah, come in, I guess."

Rachel steps through the doorway into a narrow front room. Sylvia puts her index finger across her mouth to warn Rachel not to speak, then points to a nearby chair. A tall, thin woman with wild hair sticking in all directions comes round the corner into the living room.

Her intense stare bores into Rachel.

"You're the one aint' cha? Come to get them weather glasses. You found the key, so yeah' think yeah' got a right. Yah' don't know nothin'. He's my husband. Now get yourself outta' here, Nasty little thief from up the island. Knew you'd be knocking one day."

Sylvia, whose back is to the old woman, nods to Rachel and points to the door. Sylvia follows her out and carefully shuts the door behind her.

Rachel shivers. "What's going on?"

"Can't talk now. I'll meet you in the Blue Cafe on Main St. at 4."

***

Their table in the corner, beside the window and is covered with a faded blue cloth and between them a floating candle swims in a chipped ceramic bowl.

Sylvia lifts her teacup and takes a sip, puts it down. Then she takes another long slurp of tea.

"I don't know how to say this except to come right out with it. Nina's my mom. She is your dad's second wife. I think you are seventeen. I am your half-sister, three years younger. You've come to the right place. We've been expecting you. Nina is really nasty, vengeful and crazy. When she first learned about the glasses, she kept trying to steal

32

them from Ralph. She thought she could market them and make some money. But the glasses figured out how to fool her and they kept returning themselves to where she had taken them from. They would never stay in her possession. This made her even more angry, and she would accuse us of stealing them from her. We would laugh about it because it was all so crazy. That's why Dad left her and went to live on the beach. She was so crazy about a lot of things. We kept in touch without Nina knowing. Even though he knew he was dying, he thought it better to be cold and hungry sometimes, than live with her. I insisted he go, as I couldn't stand how she treated him. He didn't want to leave me alone with her. I insisted, so he finally left."

All Rachel could say is, "Poor Ralph." Her mind is whirling with so many emotions-so many questions. Some questions are being answered. Then it clicks. Ralph put her through the search for the truth about the glasses and her grandfather, but really what he had wanted most was for the sisters to know and love one another.

"You are my sister!" She takes Sylvia's hand across the table. Sylvia grabs Rachel's hands in hers. Sylvia's face is etched with hope and love. Rachel saw worry and sadness there too. *Too young for so much trouble*, she thinks. *She is like the old souls the hippies talk about.*

There is a few minutes of silence between them. Rachel stares mindlessly into the votive candle.

"You'll want to understand about "Windless Lane," if you have a curious mind like me."

"Yes totally! Also do you know how to make the glasses change the weather. Did Ralph teach you?"

"One day the glasses, with my help, scattered a windstorm whirling in the town out and over the sea. The wind had been knocking over trees and power lines. The words one speaks while they have the glasses on have a huge effect on how the glasses function. Kind of like how abracadabra works with a magic wand but more complicated. I happened to say, while standing in the middle of this storm with the glasses on, that I wished there would never again be any wind again on out street. They took me at my word. This was the first time Dad -our dad- had let me try to control any weather. Before this I only watched him work. I felt so guilty about what I had done, but Dad just laughed and later convinced the town council to re-name the street. All anyone may know about weather systems doesn't always apply. The glasses have very human qualities. Grandfather had said they can pierce the veils between man and God, if used properly. Don't understand that so well, but I know they are about more than changing or halting the weather."

"The v-veils," Rachel stammers. "How did Grandpa possibly make something like this! It seems to out of this world. Spacey...trippin' man." She laughs nervously at her parody.

"Only God knows how the special magical and human qualities came about when grandfather put together the glasses. As far as he knew it was just a fun project, inspired by the book he wrote for our Dad."

Rachel wants to laugh and cry with joy.

"Why did he leave the glasses to me?"

Sylvia cups her chin in her palms, leans forward and looks directly at Rachel. "He didn't. They are mine."

She echoes Rachel's thoughts from a few minutes ago.

"What he really wished for more than anything was for us to know each other. He wanted you to learn the secrets of why grandfather died and how the glasses work, but no one can use the glasses but me."

"B-ut my yellow – green eyes." Rachel protests. All her joy is gone. She feels tears welling behind her eyes. She is angry with Sylvia for stealing her joy. She is angry with herself for assuming the glasses would be hers once she found them.

"Heredity, Nothing more." Sylvia sits quietly, her thoughts veiled from Rachel's understanding. *She is too self-contained*, Rachel thinks. *It's totally okay, she tells herself. We have all summer to learn about each other.*

Rachel struggles to get a handle on feelings of jealously and love, in equal measure, for her newly found sister. She grudgingly sees the truth in what Sylvia says, and she notices that her sister's Sylvia's eyes are a beautiful sea green.

She stands up and pushes away her teacup. "What do we do from here then?"

Sylvia reaches into her backpack keeping her eye on Rachel's awed and angry expression as she slides her the glasses across the table.

"I'm lending you the glasses, 'til I see you next. You can at least have them in your possession for a few days. You are the one who has brought us together. You have a lot of guts Rachel. What do they say, Moxie? I likely would not have gone looking for you."

"I didn't know you existed until today."

"I did know about you. That's my point. I'll meet you in a few days on the beach. Take care and please don't do anything stupid."

***

Two weeks later Rachel is at work in the Port David library. She stays in a small room in the back. She stands facing the book racks, pretending to sort books, but scanning a book from Ralph's collection, one of a few that she had mistakenly donated to the library. A book on local weather systems.

"Vancouver Island has the most temperate weather in Canada."

"Reverse winds called eddies may occur at infrequent intervals close to hills or cliffs. When a low pressure system collides with a system of high pressure, reversal of wind direction can occur suddenly."

Her hands shake a little as she turns the pages of the book. She is excited to know more about this as an explanation for what happened to Grandfather Fineman. A simple weather system that the glasses were not able to overcome. Is that the reason for her grandfather flying backwards over the cliff? So simple and straightforward. Nothing to do with the glasses, except for the storm they could not overcome.

Sadness overcomes her. *I feel like a worn out old woman. I need to sit down.*

Weak and dizzy yet oddly elated, she slides to the floor leaning against the book rack. The words *I need to know. I need to know*, are pounding through her brain.

I wonder if the glasses can be used as regular glasses, if I want to read small print. Surely there is no harm in just trying it out. They will either work or they won't.

She gets up, reaches into her jeans, and removes the glasses. She places them across her nose and tries to focus on a chart with small print which explains osculation and other wind phenomena.

She finds the glasses help her read the print easily.

Her supervisor, Mrs. Dooley, walks by at the end of the aisle and notices Rachel with her nose in a book. "I didn't know you wore reading glasses. Such a surprise in someone so young. Please tell me you've finished sorting the books in these last two rows, Rachel Green." Her voice takes on a higher pitch. "Remember to use the dewy, decimal system correctly. Numbers are on the spine not on the inside of the books."

Rachel never gets a chance to look around or answer, as the shelves begin to shake and then books began falling from the shelves. A freak wind flings a book sideways at her boss, hitting her smack in the forehead and knocking her over. The others fly straight from the shelves and hit Rachel in the gut and knock her backwards into the shelf behind. This in turn makes the shelf topple backwards causing a domino effect with the shelf behind. Fortunately, they were near the back of the library and no customers were behind this shclf.

Rachel lies stunned on the floor surrounded by scattered broken books. The glasses glow red beside her on the floor. "The glasses are angry," she blurts. Her boss struggles to stand and looks at her oddly. A nasty raised bruise is erupting on Mrs. Dooley's forehead.

"I'm so sorry." Rachel takes her hand and leads her to a chair. "I am so-so sorry."

"No No- not your fault dear. You couldn't have caused this. Sometimes we have oddly timed weather on the island. Are you okay? Spilled books can easily be picked up. Let's see what has happened in the rest of the library. Let's make sure the others are okay. You'll have to stay late to help clean up."

Rachel is speechless. She brushes back a few strands of flyaway hair, nods. She smiles hesitantly.

Mrs. Dooley hurries towards the front of the library and then turns back to speak to Rachel.

"I hope you didn't break your glasses, dear. Such an unusual colour. It's a wonder you can see through them at all. I must check on the customers."

***

News of the library's storm spreads quickly through the streets of the small town.
"Why would it just happen inside the library and not on the streets of the town?"
"Quirky."
"Spooky. Real spooky man."
"Maybe there's a fault under the library no one knew about."
"Mighty short fault, I'd say."
"The word fault implies an earthquake. It wasn't an earthquake because there's no fault"
"Yeah, Maybe it was the fault of something or someone else. Fault. Get it, Fault."
"I get it."

***

The next day Rachel sits alone in her room talking to the glasses, which are on the table in front of her. They catch the rays of sunlight shimmering through Rachel's one small window, which faces the delivery lane in back of the library.

"I am such a screw up. You know, don't you? Somehow you know. I don't think anyone will figure that bit out. Sylvia will know the whole story by now. I don't have the courage to go to the house on Windless Lane and talk to her. Nina will scream and curse and shake her long pointy fingers at me. Sylvia will flip out. I don't blame her. I'll wait and meet her on the beach in a few days. I can return the glasses and be done with this. My mom was right. You do have a life of your own. Maybe you aren't evil, but you are a trickster. It's amazing I or Mrs. Dooley didn't get more seriously hurt. It's a wonder she didn't fire me. Then again maybe not."

"So now you understand the glasses are only a tool."

"Sylvia! What-t-How did you get in here?"

She stood by the door. A grim expression masked her face.

"Never mind, you're coming with me. Now! Bring the glasses."

***

Rachel and Sylvia sit on a log in a forest hollow east of town. They are surrounded by skunk cabbage and sword ferns. Sitka spruce and giant redwoods surround them. Silky rain falls softly.

Rachel is momentarily caught up in the timeless peace of the forest.

"Do you want to see the glasses work? Give them to me."

Sylvia takes the glasses lovingly in her hands, then places them carefully in her lap and speaks some soft words to them Rachel could not make out. When she finishes speaking, she puts them on, stands and faces the forest of trees behind them.

Almost instantly the weather switches from a nourishing rain to a hot summer's day. The warm sun filters through the trees drying the ground and surrounding plant life almost immediately. Sylvia is completely dried off and warm like the forest and plants around her. Rachel is still wet and shivering. Her soggy strands of hair drip dirty water onto her clothes.

"Okay. I get it. The glasses are still angry. That's why I'm sitting here still soaking wet and you are completely dry."

"No. Not the glasses. They are not angry! Just me. I am so done with you for totally not listening to me when I asked you not to put on the glasses. They are mirrors of human reality. Don't you see? The glasses only mirror our changing states of mind."

"I didn't tell them to knock the books off the shelves in the library and bruise my boss's forehead," Rachel protested.

"How were you feeling that day in the library?"

"Maybe a little bit excited about possibly finding out why Grandfather was blown back over the cliff. She hesitated and looked away, realizing with a long sigh, Sylvia was right once again. "Okay, Okay…" She grabs a clump of her long hair and squeezed droplets onto the ground. "A little rebellious and angry because Dad gave you the glasses instead of me. I wasn't thinking straight because of what I has just found out about why grandfather died. I wanted to use them to read a chart in dad's weather book."

"Go home, dry off and think about all this."

Sylvia strides out of the forest, leaving Rachel standing in the glade. Soaked, sorry and alone.

She is still, shivering in her lonely spot under a Sitka tree when she hears what sounds like rustling in the bushes and footsteps nearing the edge of the clearing. Nina appears before her, like a phantom in a long black cloak. Bits of twigs and scattered leaves are stuck to her clothing and protrude from her spiky hair like a demented witch.

Rachel stares in horror. "Where did you come from?"

"Where did I come from? I followed you and your sister. Yah talked her into giving you the glasses... didn't'cha. I knew you were a troublemaker since I first laid eyes on you. Yah better git on outa this town before I put a spell on you...Like I did your Dad and Grandpa."

"Wha' what do you mean. You put a spell on Ralph and Grandpa?"

"Ralph was easy- too easy. But yer grandpa, I had to work harder to figure him out. Ya don't think he fell of that cliff just cause the wind turned do yah?" Instead of cackling in triumph like a witch, Nina stands motionless, staring into Rachel's eyes. So close they could touch. Menacing and motionless.

Rachel was shivering, not from cold but from fright. She began treading backwards through the clearing away from Nina.

"What did you do to Grandpa?" She was poised to turn and run, but not til she heard Nina's reply.

Then began the cackle. Piercing, shrill, like wind through a long, lonely tunnel. Rachel runs through the hollow and out on to the road. The sound is still ringing in her ears when she arrives at the centre of town and throws herself down on a bench, panting She is choking with fear and loathing.

Sylvia finds her sometime later.

"I'm taking you home. Nina will have to deal with it."

"Nina, no not Nina. Please!! She came through the woods after you left me. She was so close, scaring me. Saying she put a spell on your Dad and Grandpa."

"Oh really, No. She just likes to sound mean. She DOES sound mean, and it gets to you after a while, but it's just words. She's harmless really."

"Sylvia, listen to me. She wants the glasses. Somethings going on."

"I need to get you some dry clothes. You're a shivering wreck. Shouldn't have left you there on you own. You're imagining things."

She grabs Rachel by the arm and pulls her along the street towards her home on Windless Lane.

Sylvia led Rachel to the back room. Nina screamed and pounded on the door.

"You can't bring that brat in here. I'm telling you!" More pounding, like the door would splinter.

Sylvia found a nightgown for Rachel, took off her soggy clothes and made her get into bed.

"This is the safest place for you now. Nina's on a rampage. I need to see if I can calm her down. Sleep well."

Rachel slcpt soundly for the next few hours. In the middle of the night, she woke with a start to see what looked like a tall shadow of Nina, wearing a black hood and looming across her bed. Terrified, she turned to the wall. She heard a voice that she couldn't quite place. Like Nina's but something was different. More sinister. A younger voice?

"You better be off in the morning. I looked after the other two and I can look after you. You be listenin' careful now to my words, you little thief from up the island."

Rachel lies very still. No words are possible. Her throat muscles are frozen. Then she turns around quickly and tears the hood off the looming figure. There stands Sylvia, frozen, speechless at being so easily found out.

But Rachel isn't speechless, she is horrified. "How could you, Sylvia, Really Sylvia! How could you? I thought we were sisters. You are not my sister or my friend. You are horrible, creepy and mean just like your mother."

Rachel rushes from the room, grabbing her bag of clothes, pushing Sylvia aside.

Sylvia tumbles to the floor. She calls after Rachel.

"Wait a minute. I don't mean any harm. Just a joke."

"The little thief from up the island? I'm done!"

She waits in her room behind the library until it opens at 9:00 am. She quickly gathers her things, locks the door behind her. Trembling at the curtains, she imagines shadows of hooded figures in the dim light from the streetlamp and in the waking dawn.

"I have to go home. I can't work here anymore," she tells Mrs. Dooley. "The storm in the library is still freaking me out," she lied.

"Freaking you out? What strange language you young people use nowadays. If you must go, I can't stop you. Oh dear, such a shame. Good Luck dear." Her voice rises in this final goodbye. Rachel turns to wave just as she manages catch the revolving door before it turns away.

And with that Rachel is gone. She gets off the bus and trudges up the dirt and gravel road to home determined never to return to Port David.

There were many talks with her mother in the waning weeks of this North Island summer.

She didn't tell her mother everything. She couldn't say anything about her strange encounter with Nina, in the clearing and then the horrible threats from Sylvia in the night. There was the bewildering new knowledge that Nina had maybe put a spell on Grandpa and Ralph. She didn't know anymore whether she could even trust her own sister. Had Nina also put some kind of a lesser spell on Sylvia? Is that why she was hanging onto the glasses so fiercely? Did Sylvia lie to her or omit the truth as her mom had done?

One afternoon mother and daughter are sitting in the garden.

Rachel is leaning on the table. Her hair is dirty and tangled and she is wearing a shirt hastily rescued from the dirty laundry basket.

Emily leans towards her daughter, coffee cup in hand.

"Why did you leave your job so suddenly? Something is terribly wrong. I can feel it. Did you have a falling out with Sylvia?"

Rachel is alarmed that her mom has sensed the truth. Not wanting to show her hand just yet, she sits up straight, looks directly at her mom and answers.

"Not exactly. But she is keeping the glasses in her possession. I wonder why? She says Ralph wanted her to have them. I'm not sure this is the truth. Not sure of much anymore."

"You need to rest dear. When you're ready we can sort things out together."

Ignoring her mother's advice, Rachel blurts out.

"Why do you keep so much from me. Why do I have to go through so much pain!"

"This is life. Life is pain. Do you really think you're the only one going through stuff?" Emily hesitates. Bewildered, she looks pleadingly at her daughter. So troubled and so defiant. She softens her tone.

"I wanted the glasses out of my sight, so I asked Ralph to take them away. I didn't honestly know he'd put any clues upstairs. When you told me that the other day, I was surprised to say the least. He certainly did that on the sly."

 Rachel stands up and kicks at the legs of the empty chair between them, knocking it sideways.

"Why should I believe that flimsy excuse?"

"I kept things from you. I never lied."

"What's the difference?"

Emily walks stiffly over to Rachel. She is racked with guilt and misgivings.

She picks up the chair Rachel had kicked and sits in it beside her daughter. "I have been wrong. Wanting to protect you. But you are strong willed. I should have known you wouldn't take no for an answer."

 The wind begins to blow softly. Rachel's eyes glisten with anger, but also a glint of excitement.

Emily smiles, trying to regain Rachel's confidence. "I will tell you the story. Since you have been on this search, it's only right now to explain what I know."

Emily lights a smoke and moves her chair back from the table.

So Emily reveals it was Nina who had become involved with Ralph and ruined their marriage. "She cast an evil spell, of a sort, over him and he was pulled away from the life we had loved here together. Pulled away from you, my child. I just wanted to protect you. You are right, the time for protecting you is finished. Ralph and I fought bitterly, after the horrible accident when you were ten. We argued and accused each other of whatever came to mind, even after eight years of being apart! I guess I was still jealous. When I asked why he had left me for that woman, he said only that she was like a cry from another world that he needed to explore. "Not good enough," I screamed. "You had a good life here with me and Rachel. Weren't we enough for you!" Eventually, he agreed to take the glasses, but as you told me, he left the clues in the attic for you to find. He wanted you to know your family and he was so right. I wanted to keep you from his new family and all that crazy stuff. And then later, whcn all went so wrong, I just didn't know how to begin to explain."

"So, I had a father I never knew. All those years you kept this beautiful man from me. I wanted to know him, mum. He was-is- my dad! I have a sister I would have liked to know sooner. All the years I wondered and wept for Grandfather. As a small child maybe, but after Grandpa's accident? I don't know, mom, how to just accept this now."

"You were too fragile, and I guess I was too." Emily, tears streaming from her eyes, beseeching forgiveness, puts her arm around her daughter and tries to give her a hug.

Rachel resists. She sits firmly against the back of the chair looking sadly at her mother.

"Even though she's not my blood, she is your sister and I have to accept that."

This concession, which she would have welcomed only a month or so ago, is now sadly confusing to Rachel.

She turns and walks quickly to her room, without acknowledging her mom's new understanding. She lies on her bed. She cries and mumbles to herself, then she falls into an exhausted, restless sleep. In her dream the doorbell is ringing over and over. First, she sees her grandpa, standing outside ringing the bell. Then he pulls the glasses out of his raincoat, puts them on and goes back down the steps. Then Ralph is there as a child, reaching up to ring the bell. He is wearing a green corduroy school uniform, consisting of a suit jacket and sweater and short pants, just like the picture of him in "Ralph and the Golden Glasses." He is clutching his treasured copy of the book. Then the dream flips and it's Sylvia standing on the steps. The ringing gets louder. She wakes and stumbles to the door. Sylvia is standing on the step looking tired but determined.

"Can I come in Rachel?"

She steps back. Standing inside the open door and having no idea how to react, she combs her fingers through her tangled hair. "Holy Crap- you were just in my dream ringing the doorbell for 20 min. Where's your cloak and hood- Forget it at home? Nina using it today?"

"Holy Crap -What?"

"Never mind," Rachel says testily. "Come in I guess." She turns to look back through to the kitchen. Mom must be tending to the horses."

Gathering her thoughts, Rachel points Sylvia to a chair in the living room. "How and why are you here?" She speaks curtly.

"The how doesn't matter. I really need to talk to you."

"Everyone wants to talk. Let's hear it. I know, Oh yes. You're sorry you lied. Line up with the rest of them."

"I get it. You're angry with me."

"Amazing deduction, Sister! Who has the glasses now Sylvia? Your crazy witch of a mother? Answer the question. More to the point. Who's more deceitful, you or Nina?"

"How did you know the glasses weren't left to me?"

"Nina may be nuts, but she's not stupid. Why would she come after me, if she didn't believe or know the glasses were actually left to me by Ralph? You brought me to Windless Lane, knowing she

56

would come after me so then you could pretend to be her and drive me away. What do you really want Sylvia? Why did you come here? Why don't you head back out the door? Go back to Port David- to your crazy mother- and leave me and my mom to ourselves."

The front screen bangs shut. Emily stands in the entrance between kitchen and living room. She gestures a welcome to Sylvia.

Sylvia is standing by the chair. Perplexed. She picks up her backpack and shifts it over her shoulder.

"You must be Sylvia. Stay awhile. Welcome to our home. Rachel, make us some tea. I will read you girl's tea leaves. This is really so exciting."

"Mom, she doesn't want tea! For God's sake! I want her to leave. She's not welcome here."

Sylvia drops her backpack and plunks down in the chair once again.

"Make up your mind you guys." She looks embarrassed, slightly amused, glancing back and forth between mother and daughter.

"What's up with you Rachel? I thought you wanted to know your sister. Here she is in our living room!"

"I'll make tea." Rachel sighs wearily and retreats to the kitchen. "You talk to her, mom."

Emily and Sylvia stare at one another, not knowing where to begin.

"I'm very glad to--"

"I'm so sorry."

"Sorry about what- You've come all this way. Dear child you must be tired from your travels. Rest awhile."

Ignoring Emily, Sylvia carries on.

"Rachel doesn't want me here, but before I go, I have to say, I lied to Rachel. I'm here to settle things."

Rachel cringes as she listens by the doorway. Not able to bear the frustration, Rachel lurches into the living room with the tea tray, spilling most of it onto the tray. Emily carefully edges the tray away from her daughter's hands and places it on the table.

Rachel stands by Sylvia's chair, her arms folded tightly against her gut, trying to stem her anxiety. She is taunt with anger.

"I thought you were my friend. I thought we were kindred spirits. I guess that's just another stupid, hippie dream. You did a trick with the glasses to make me think I was the one who'd messed up. Can you imagine me hearing from Nina that she had put a spell on Dad and Grandpa? This coming after I was left alone in the woods? Later you dragged me home with you. Nina came to haunt me in the night. But it wasn't Nina. It was YOU creeping around my room. You want this. You want rid of me too."

"Then why am I here? Why would I hike to the end of the island, if I still want to be rid of you?"

"The glasses were meant for me," Rachel rebuffs stubbornly.

"No, not exactly."

"Tell me another story."

Emily is sitting in her chair, eyes keen, focused on what Sylvia is saying.

"LET her tell you Rachel. I want to hear this."

"Okay explain yourself Sylvia. Explain yourself. Is this all true, what Rachel is saying? Was I right all along to keep her from you and your family?"

"I did do most of those things and I am horribly sorry. I was so jealous that the glasses were not left to me. I did not get Nina to haunt you though. I had nothing to do with that. That was horrible. That's what I have to live with all the time- a crazy mother- she is really nuts and she thinks she is a witch. She thinks she has all these powers. She works on spells in her room. She practises from a book and has all these potions on her dresser. She thinks her so called witch powers and the help of the glasses were what blew Grandpa off the cliff. The twist in the wind, like you discovered for yourself, overcame the power of the glasses. That's all. There is one more thing."

"What now. Haven't you done enough?"

"This is partly why I am here. The glasses weren't left to me or to you."

Breathless silence fills the room.

Sylvia sits on the edge of the chair and unzips her
backpack, carefully removing the glasses.
She looks straight ahead at Emily, then hands her
the glasses.

"Me! He left the glasses to me?"

Sylvia says nothing. She pulls another piece of
paper from her pack. She passes it to Emily.

Emily's hands shake as she reads:

> Emily, my wife. My only true love.
> I know that now but there is no time
> left. Only time to say, please look
> after the girls. I leave the girls and
> the glasses in your care, so that
> when you are ready you may decide,
> who will inherit the glasses. My
> wish is that Rachel and Sylvia share
> the ownership, so they can work
> together, and no covetousness will
> overcome their good sense.
> Forever love,
> Your husband Ralph.

Emily sits in shock. Rachel is feeling overwhelmed too. Sylvia sits quietly seeing their need to process what has happened. Emily is the first to speak.

"I will treasure this token of love. She folds her hands over the letter, holding it close to her heart. Thank you, Sylvia."

"I want to try and make it up to you and Rachel. My foolishness- my selfish stupidity. May I stay here until I figure out what I'm going to do? I don't want to go back to Port David. I know I have no right to ask because of the trouble I've caused. But if you let me stay for a bit--" She hangs her head. Her hair hangs in wisps covering her face. She looks up at Emily, her face hopeful, sorry and sad.

Emily interrupts. "You may stay the night. We'll all talk more in the morning. Now get yourself upstairs. Bedroom at the top of the stairs on the right. Goodnight, sleep well."

Thinking she'd seen the last of Sylvia for the night, Rachel was dumbfounded when Sylvia suddenly turned back towards them before going upstairs. Sylvia's face contorts with anger. *How can one person's mood change so fast*, she wonders.

"You, you two think you're so perfect. I'm telling you the other reason I came here. Emily or Rachel, you could have told me. How do you think I found out my Dad died. In the newspaper! The local rag! Do you know how that made me feel? You never thought for one moment about me. Just the glasses. Always the glasses. No wonder I wanted them They were all I had left. There it was, his name and picture in the obituary column. How could you be so uncaring?" She looks over at Emily with a withering resentful sneer. Emily is staring at her, frozen and speechless, from the middle of the room.

Sylvia walks slowly up to the first landing then faces the two women. "I'll stay the night and be out of your face in the morning." She disappears down the dark hallway.

After Sylvia disappears, Rachel glares across at her mother.

"Do you think letting her stay was a safe thing to do. Really mom? Are you all in love with Ralph again? That's ridiculous! He's kind and wonderful but he's dead- Remember?"

"Ralph had faith in all of us. That transcends death. Where's yours?

"Faith in her. Really? After what she did? She betrayed me mom."

"Oh, get over yourself! Aren't you so precious and perfect."

"Mom-You've sure changed your tune. She scared me half to death. She lied. How can you tell me to get over myself!"

"I know you've been through a lot, but ask yourself when you're lying awake tonight. Why did she hike all the way here? She had no money and no bus-fare. No one cares for her. Think about it! She has lost her father who she adored and then is left alone with her bizarre mother. I could have sent her a letter or made a phone call to tell her what happened to her Dad and express our sympathy. It might have prevented her from doing what she did to you. Oh my God! Can we not try to show her some compassion? Why did she finally give me the Ralph's letter?"

Brow furrowed, she walks out onto the porch. Rachel follows. Emily leans over the railing, butt dangling from her mouth. She opens it to speak and the butt falls over the railing to the ground below. She turns toward Rachel.

"That's it. She was left out of the whole business of recovering Ralph's body and having him buried here, She has come to see her dad, not us! There's more than her bad acting, that is making her look so sorry and sad. Don't you see Rachel? She has no one. No wonder she is acting so strange, hanging onto the glasses like they are the only friend she has. I never thought. We have to make this up to her. Tomorrow.

I'll take your room across from Sylvia. I'll toss you down a blanket and pillow. Make sure the door is locked. I hope you sleep well. You are my loving child always, no matter how frustrated I am with you, myself, others or the situation."

Before her mom turns to climb the stairs, Rachel looks her square in the eye and places her hands lightly on her mom's shoulders.

"You are right. I can't deny that Sylvia was neglected in all this. You are my rock, mum, my best friend, despite our different way of seeing things."

Emily takes her in a hug and this time Rachel does not pull away.

In spite of reconciling somewhat with her mom, Rachel does not sleep. She cannot close her eyes, but to see the hooded shape of Nina or Sylvia looming over the lumpy couch. She had not known then, that she even had a sister. But her mom had known. She realizes this with a shock wave to her heart. *We have all been living in our own world. Time to focus on each other instead of the glasses.*

Sylvia stays at Cliff-Side for the remaining weeks of the summer. She helps tend the goats, weeds the gardens, and brushes, feeds and helps clean up after the horses. Rachel eventually offers her a turn on the old mare, Sally. They ride bareback, Rachel in front, down the dusty road. They plan to visit Rachel's favourite meadow, but Sally has another idea. As they near the fork in the road, she snorts, shakes her mane, turns and trots left heading towards the family cemetery. She halts in between the memorial for Grandpa Fineman and headstone for Ralph.

"Look at you," Rachel nuzzles Sally. "You're my smart girl. I have ridden you here a few times, but still, I didn't think of coming here. Look at you! You brought us to the right place."

Sylvia looks at Sally with a shocked amazement. Then her focus shifts to the gravestones.

The girls stand quietly, thinking their own thoughts. Then Sylvia kneels in front of Ralph's gravestone. Tears fall across her cheeks. She brushes them away. "I love you dad."

Then she sits on the concrete bench beside her sister. "Your mom has said nothing to me, She hasn't apologized. Nada. Not a word."

"She will talk to you. I know her. She doesn't rush at things like me."

The girls slowly begin to confide their joy and heartache to each other, unsure at first of how to be the true sisters they were so excited about being, only a month ago.

Before Sylvia returns to Port David, Emily and the girls talk. Well, Emily talks.

Emily sits at the kitchen table with the girls on either side. She looks directly at Sylvia, her posture unyielding.

"You will return to Port David tomorrow, Sylvia. I have arranged for you to stay in the back room at the library where Rachel stayed. You will have a job there after school three days a week and on Saturdays. It's all arranged with Mrs. Dooley. You are free to live your own life and not be burdened so much, by your difficult mother. Now, having said that, you must look in on your mother. Make sure she has groceries and whatever she needs. I would advise you not to talk of the glasses or their whereabouts. But you likely know this already. If she causes trouble or there is a problem, you need help with get in touch with me right away. You are not alone anymore. We ARE your family. I am sorry I didn't know you in your growing up years. I will help out with money where I can. You must not cause any grief to your family, or I'll have to make other arrangements. I think you are past these things. You know what you did to Rachel. You have hurt your sister and me as well. We are both trying to understand the terrible loneliness you must have felt when your father died, and no one considered you in the process at all. We thought only of ourselves and about the glasses. Those damn glasses. They have had a hold on us. We have all made stupid mistakes, but we are not going to carry them around with us."

Not sure exactly how she feels, but not wanting to sound greedy or ungrateful, Sylvia replies.” I am grateful to you Emily. I feel more like you really are becoming my real mom now.” And then the dig came.

“If Rachel doesn’t mind sharing.”

Rachel accepts the dig and responds.

 “I see that smirk, Sylvia. You are becoming more like your old self again. Well, not too much like your old self.”

“Touché,” Sylvia smirks again, her green eyes twinkling. “I guess I deserve that.”

“Okay girls. Enough!” Emily clears her throat. “Ahem, about the glasses.” The sisters sit up in rapt attention. “I will hang onto the glasses for the time being. Later we will decide how to use and to share them. We don’t want them ever again to be the cause of unhappiness or contention. Please don’t ask where they are, or I will know then that you don’t respect or understand what we need to do.”

***

Sylvia began work, as was arranged, in the Port David library. Mrs. Dooley sometimes frets to Sylvia about the day of the strange storm. Sylvia would agree with her that it really was an odd occurrence. She would ponder how close Mrs. Dooley really was to the truth of the situation.

"That poor child, Rachel. She peers down at Sylvia, her frosty, styled head of hair framing her sharp features and her glasses hanging from the end of her nose, she's your sister, I think. She wore the strangest looking pair of glasses I've ever seen. Do you know anything about those glasses? She was so frightened and feeling guilty thinking she'd somehow caused the problem. Rachel quit her job a few days later. Poor dear. Not her responsibility. Who can control the weather, I ask you?"

"Who indeed," Sylvia smiles.

***

One August afternoon, shortly after Rachel's high school graduation, Sylvia and Rachel are relaxing in wooden chairs under the gnarly apple-tree, behind Rachel's house. They talk about everything and nothing. Emily brings them tea, then leaves them to themselves. They chat about plans for their education, aspiring careers and their current or their would-be boyfriends. Emily, coffee in hand, watches the girls from the shadow of the porch.

Rachel brings up the glasses because she is considering taking climatology studies at university. She wants Sylvia's opinion as to the courses she wishes to take and so on.

"I am beginning to understand before enrolling at the university," Rachel begins, "All the climatology, geography, weather science in the world cannot explain how the glasses became infused with magic as Grandpa Forrest fashioned them. I now know that as you do, they are a mirror of our human feelings and also a scientific tool to control the weather. The world is not ready for such a tool. They teach us about ourselves. I am so glad we got through that crazy time a few summers ago."

Rachel is taller than her sister and slimmer with long legs. She looks at her sister envying her thick hair, her sea green eyes and her fuller figure. *Better than my red, frizzy mop and my glassy, yellow-green eyes.* She sighs.

The perfume of the ripening apples and the wildflowers in the meadow beyond, dances in the breeze around their chairs. Sylvia doesn't respond directly to what Rachel has said. "Oh yeah me too. Glad we got through that time. Remember that day in the woods. I was such a bag, so self righteous."

Rachel nods graciously although in the back of her mind, she still occasionally feels the sting of Sylvia's deceptions. *I wonder why this came up. I guess I brought up the subject first, but only to talk of the glasses in connection to what I want to study. They weren't your glasses to begin with,* she thinks. Instead, she replies with these words.

"So young and foolish. You were 14 and alone with your mom. No wonder. No one has a handle on life at 14, or at 17 for that matter."

Sylvia answers quickly, "Hah! Yes, you're right. We're still young and foolish with many more mistakes to look forward to."

She throws back her head and laughs.

"You throw your head back when you laugh, just like Ralph used to."

"Speaking of glasses, has your mum decided yet what will happen with the glasses?"

This remark as with the former, coming from nowhere rattles Rachel. She stands up with her back to her sister, stretches her legs and looks away. She focuses on the horses grazing in the meadow close by. *Sally is getting quite a sway back. Dear kind Sally, getting old,* she thinks sadly. Then she recalls her mother last summer, just before Sylvia left Cliff-side, telling the girls firmly not to ask about the glasses. Rachel doesn't know what to think. She wrings her hands, then turns and sits again.

"Did I say something wrong?"

"No, it's fine, I just wanted to stand up and stretch. We never talk of the glasses anymore." It's up to mom – Remember?"

"Yes," Sylvia blushes, "You're right. We have other things to think about."

Rachel notices a sly smirk behind her sister's blush. She shivers and clears her throat. "Shall we have more tea. I'll read your leaves."

"That sounds like fun."

***

Emily, eyes and ears alert to the nature of the chatter and to the occasional shriek of laughter coming from the garden, leans against the porch and sighs, as she absently discards her cigarette ashes onto the floor of the deck.

In the sweetness of a summer afternoon, the young women's mingled laughter floats in the redolent air around the apple tree.

Eileen lives in Clearwater, B.C., by the North Thompson River where she enjoys walking the dog. She has a messy garden in the backyard in which she putters about happily.

Contact Eileen through Celticfrog Publishing at celticfrog@live.com

Other Published Works by Eileen Bell

Selkirk to Sagebrush 2021

River-land and other Poems 2020

The Keeper of the Shell 2019

Stories available in various Anthology's

Books available on Amazon.

Eileen Bell is a regular contributor of stories and poems to the New Author's Journal published quarterly.

For other soon to be published works please refer to CelticFrogPublishing.com/Eileen-Bell.

9 781989 092712